ROGUE

L. F. GOBIN

'I spit in
the eye of
Satan'

EXISTENCE

As a young human, I had led a troubled life. At the age of sixteen, I fled the family home only to find myself homeless and avoiding the authorities. Recklessly, I flirted with death, allowing myself to be used and abused in exchange for just a little change, a little food, or a little shelter. I entered a world of darkness and despair, often contemplating thoughts of suicide. Eventually, I made the decision to end my pain and my existence. Standing on the edge of a dilapidated bridge, ready to plunge into the abyss, my suffering was a beacon for all that was dark to hear.

That fateful night, a shadow loomed over my cowering form. Paralysis overtook my body and unimaginable pain followed as my blood was taken from me. I had dreamt for death, so death had come for me. I welcomed its dark embrace and the release it would offer me. I silently thanked whatever powers that may be for this opportunity. No memories flashed before my eyes. I saw nothing. It was bliss.

It was not meant to be. I had been mercilessly deceived. My maker left me for dead in a vomitous alleyway cloying for breath. Not only did I still live, I was also faced with a thirst that I could not quench. A hunger that I had never felt before, even during my days of human starvation, took hold of me. Its presence was so extreme that it seemed to materialise into a being of some sort, hounding me to no extremes. I staggered to the nearest food source – maggot-infested leftovers – and consumed all I could until I became sick. The anguish was so great that I could not walk without stumbling. I was blinded by searing pain, deafened by the ferocity of it, and incapacitated by its incredible strength. The grasping claws of hunger dug into my flesh, twisting my insides relentlessly. It burned and I did not know how to extinguish its rage.

Just when I was at my wit's end, I had the most bizarre experience. I spotted a rat in my peripheral and my vision sharpened, zoning in on the rodent. I heard its heart beating as if it had been amplified a thousand times and a musty odour filled my nostrils. My muscles tensed, preparing to spring. I pounced onto the filthy sewer rat and before I had a second to comprehend what was happening, I sunk my teeth into its grimy, writhing body. Lush blood, thick and velvety, flowed through me, providing me with just a minuscule amount of sustenance. Craving more of this warm liquid, I drank another and another.

The high was only temporary; the comedown devastating and punishing.

I needed another hit.

I slunk around in search of something larger, and ultimately, something more satisfying, believing that it would tame my deadly appetite. My initial thought was a cat or a dog, but what I found was so much sweeter. As I sat clutching my hollow stomach, I was approached by an unsavoury man with vile thoughts. Mistaking me for a drunk, he attempted to coax me with alcohol. Now that I had tasted blood, liquor held no appeal. I had once used my body to entice others into giving me money, but now I demanded so much more. Something that money could not buy, and you could not put a value on. My vision centered on the vein throbbing in his neck.

It whispered sweet promises of delicious nourishment.

Startled by my sudden movement, he could do little to resist. I bit at his neck at first, wildly missing my mark, causing deep gashes on his soiled neck. He fought me, but I persisted, and ultimately, he failed. I was rewarded with an ecstasy so great that I immediately became addicted. I drank so greedily and selfishly that his death passed by unnoticed. Only when his blood ran cold, did I realise I was drinking from a corpse.

One hit was all it took.

One taste.

Addicted to this heady substance, I sought to find more. In all my human years, I had never found a drug so potent and pure. Only another kill could satisfy this crushing need. I was a junkie, an addict, hooked on the thrill of the hunt. I went on a murderess rampage, draining every unfortunate soul living on the fringes of human society. I no longer saw them as beings with any value. In my eyes, they were both vulgar and easy to ensnare with their slow, cumbersome movements and careless behaviour. Far from the apex predator they desired to be, they were easy prey. They were nothing but blood.

Over time, the bloodlust settled, and gorging myself until I was ready to burst did not compel me as it had before. I had entered a strange pupal-like stage of vampire hood. What I was going to metamorphosise into, I had no clue. What horror awaited me? I struggled to see the point of it all, especially if my life would be one of regret. I had once had family and friends, but when I closed my eyes, I could no longer see their faces. I could not recollect my reason for leaving them. What terrible thing had they done to me?

The less I fed, the more I remembered, the more human I felt and the more horrified I became as I recalled my disturbing and ruinous actions. Fleeting visions of my family played repetitively like a continuous film reel. Memories of my mother, father, and brother evoked unwanted feelings – feelings I thought long dead overcame me. Yes, I had loved and been loved once. I longed for that warm feeling once again. The bloodlust confused me and made me believe that I was in love with the chase, the hunt , and the kill. I needed to wean myself off of its deadly grip and free myself of the burning need to kill.

I wandered aimlessly until I realised that my legs were leading me along a path I had walked many times. I let my intuition guide me. When I finally stopped, I was breathless, weakened by the lack of blood. I saw an open window, beckoning me and inviting me inside. Once inside, my strength faded further, and I hoped that someone would save me. My surroundings faded as I fell into a dreamless sleep, but I was awakened by a creature who had been alerted to my presence. A dog, who had once been my companion, affectionately nuzzled me. I held its warm body, comforted by its ignorance of my past actions. My hunger returned with a vengeance when I felt its beating heart and its life force flowing strongly. A dark crimson mist descended, and my teeth found no resistance as they broke the skin, and my mouth filled with sweet, thick blood.

Two familiar humans entered the room. I barely had time to register their reactions because I was blinded by a rage so sudden and strong. I did not understand from where it came. I just saw red.

What followed was beyond evil.

Those, who had once loved me, were no more.

My parents lay in a pool of their own blood on the bedroom floor.

Killed.

Not for their blood, but for sport.

Before I could comprehend the consequences of my depraved actions, my brother burst through the door, having heard all the commotion. The moment he saw the carnage, he dropped to his knees and wept. A feral voice urged me to kill and feed on his grieving, innocent flesh, but something inside me prevented it. An overwhelming urge to escape this terrible scene convinced me to flee the site.

Only one destiny awaited me.

Death by my own hand.

I tried to end my life in any way that I could. Every possible way one might try, I tried. Burning, only to find that it hurt like I had walked through hell itself; driving a wooden stake through one's own heart, only to realise that I am heartless; hurtling off a building, only to find that I am unbreakable; inhaling gas and noxious fumes, only to find that it has no effect; taking a drug overdose only to discover that it causes a mere, allergic reaction. Every attempt resulted in catastrophic failure.

Even my attempt to decapitate myself failed miserably. Reduced to a bloody pulp, I still regenerated; impossibly so. No matter how I hoped for the rats to feast on my flesh as I lay wounded and rotting in their cesspit of a home, they would not come. No matter how much I prayed for humans to find me, fear me, and finish me, they did not come to hunt me down.

Running out of options, I decided to deprive myself of the one thing I needed: blood. It almost had the desired effect as it weakened me greatly, so I crawled out in my pathetic state to expose myself to the sun, believing that combining blood loss with exposure would mark my demise. Drained of my bodily fluid, I lay in the gutter, unable to move. Pain overwhelmed my senses. I had only succeeded in creating a new kind of prison for myself – trapped in a body that could not move, and tortured by my own thoughts and dreams.

And nightmares.

When I ignored the bloodlust entirely, I was plagued by a grief so great, a sorrow so pure, that hollowness took up permanent residence in my lost soul. I waited and waited long hard years, yet death did not come. I did not heal. I was a living, breathing corpse. Abandoned by every entity known to man, I was destined to suffer alone.

Even hell would not have me.

ILLUMINATION

I was woken from my fitful slumber by a voice that I could not hear and thoughts that were not my own. In the darkness, something or someone called to me. There was a familiar feeling about the presence that I detected. I had an overwhelming urge to find a purpose other than wishing for death. Although I deserved it, I could no longer take this endless suffering that yielded no result.

I could barely move my decayed body, so I called out to the night and it answered. Strangely, as if my dark prayer had been heard, a rat crawled through a crevice in the rubble, followed by a stray cat in pursuit of the unfortunate being. It nudged aside brick after brick to find its tasty morsel. As the flea-infested rat scurried over my fingers, I grabbed it in a sudden burst of desperation. Its pursuer fled, frightened by my sudden movement. I drained the small crushed body dry. It brought me just enough strength to reach out and grab the next one.

With all my might, I detached myself from the muck and the human waste. It was hard to tell where my body began and the grime ended. I dragged my skeletal frame through the dirt until it grated against the rough, concrete ground. How my bones scraped against every crack and bump. I felt each one as if a wound split open anew, agonizingly fresh. I do not know how long it took as my sense of time was skewed. I had lost the concept of time under the bricks and rubble which had accumulated around me.

After crawling to the end of the narrow alleyway, I spotted a human passed out and slumped against the wall, oblivious to the world and begging to be released from his wretched existence. I drank my fill and his life essence shattered as he took his last, ragged breath. Then little by little the pain lessened. When I finally gathered enough strength to stand upright unaided, I immediately collapsed under the sheer weight of my own body.

God, why did you curse me so? Satan, what would you have me do? I pleaded silently to the night. I bowed my head in vain, but I was roused from my reverie by a presence, once again.

A shadowy figure stood above me, clad in a dark robe, and atop his head, a halo of light glowed. I immediately felt insignificant in this presence which exuded omnipotence, and I basked in his glory. A dark angel – Death himself – had heard my prayers and had come to end my suffering. I could not distinguish his features, as a filmy layer coated my still recovering eyes. As I blinked, my eyes adjusted to the bright fluorescent light and much to my disappointment, I saw that it was merely a streetlight. Death was, in fact, just a man.

A priest to be exact.

"My poor child. How you suffer." He spoke to me with such tenderness.

"What do you know of suffering, Father?" I said bitterly, my rasping voice cracking. It had been a number of years since I had spoken aloud. I sounded like a record littered with deep scratches, yet the man did not flinch or shy away.

"I once suffered as you did, until I found a purpose," he answered softly.

"Don't tell me – our so-called God, who abandoned and cursed me with this evil disease?"

He knelt down beside me. "This robe is but a costume which allows me to serve. I am one of you, my friend. I use my strength for good."

"You are a blood drinker? A vampire?" I asked, astounded by this discovery.

"Oh please, let's not use such crude terminology. I prefer the term, 'Nightwalker' and that is the term used by the council."

"The council?" I questioned, my confusion growing further.

"Yes, the council. It is led by our leader, Draconis."

I snorted derisively. "The dragon, I assume?"

"It is no fable. He was bitten by the last dragon." The Priest explained with conviction in his eyes because he truly believed this to be true.

"Was it not bats?" I retorted scornfully but immediately regretted my harshness. Truth or deception, there was no need for such abrasiveness as the man had a pleasant manner.

"Ah, yes. A story created by humans, but it is not so. Ancient texts speak of creatures unknown to you – great flying serpents that roamed the Earth."

Making sure to use a softer note, I asked, "With what evidence do you make such claims? There is none."

"How do you know there is none? Humans harbour more secrets than we. Imagine, for a second, if they knew about our kind? They would band together to destroy us. It is in their very nature to destroy what they do not understand, is it not? Ignorance has caused much illogical behaviour amongst humans. We are free from such things." Tilting his head; his brow furrowed, he asked, "You are strange and different. Who is your maker?"

"I have no idea," I stated, suddenly weary. I wondered how he could possibly expect me to know.

"You must see the council. We must account for every rogue and find your maker. Permission must be granted before creating a nightwalker. Your maker must be made accountable for abandoning you unless he or she has somehow perished."

"Rogue?"

"An unknown nightwalker. Just like the humans, we have records of births and deaths."

I was curious about this council as I had never encountered one like myself.
Maybe they could offer some kind of solace in my tormented existence. Maybe they could explain the reason for us or why I was made.

"But for now, come with me. You must feed."

"But you are a priest," I said numbly.

Understanding exactly what I meant, he explained, "A priest who eats like any other."

"Are you not committing a sin?"

"We have our own laws. I live by the commandments set by the council, as human texts are tainted by the bias of man. We have no need for such texts as blood tells a much more powerful story."

Holding out his hand to me, I clasped it desperately. He looked down on me in pity as he took in my worn, tattered clothing. I hated feeling weak and pathetic, but there was nothing I could do to hide my malcontent. His hand felt firm and strong as he all but lifted me off the ground. He smiled kindly at me as he waited for me to steady myself and stand independently.

"What is your name, child?"

"Aurora. What do they call you, Priest?"

"Exactly that – Priest." I could not tell if he was being facetious, so I opted for silence.

Holding an arm out in an absurdly gentlemanly gesture, he waited patiently for me to take hold of it. He made me feel like I was somebody worth living because there was no judgement of me. I latched on to it like a drug. I craved more of this attention. It was something that had been missing from my undeserved life.

He led me to a grand church with floor-to-ceiling stained glass windows. We walked alongside the seats until he opened a door hidden behind the confessional. I found myself standing in a dimly lit corridor with many doors leading to different rooms. After descending a darkened staircase, we came across another door which opened to some sort of dining room – a room that could seat a number of people.

Once seated at the grand, dark wooden table. I almost felt as if I were about to delve into a five-course meal. I had not eaten human food for many years. The thought made me snort quietly and Priest looked at me oddly. I could not recall the last time I found anything amusing.

Priest left the room briefly and returned with three small bags filled with blood, which appeared almost black in the candlelight.

"How do you like it, Aurora?"

I looked at him as if he had spoken another language.

"Fresh?"

He laughed loudly and the noise was so sudden that I almost jumped up in surprise. I felt ridiculous, once I saw the glasses he set down earlier and realised what he meant. The embarrassment felt alien to me.

Not wanting to appear dim-witted in the presence of Priest, I quickly said, "Sorry, I misunderstood. Straight from the bag is fine."

He handed it to me with laughter lingering in his face. I lowered my head, averting my vision, unable to return eye contact.

"Thank you, Priest."

He proceeded to pour the contents of his into a wine glass, which he cupped with his hands. The gesture did not quite make sense, as he could not possibly warm the stale, cold liquid with his deathly cold hands. And yet, he swished it around as if it were an exquisite, expensive wine, while I just sucked my bag dry like the uncouth vagrant I was. What he must think of me, I thought. He eyed me watchfully, but he made no comment.

When I was satiated, I could not help but lean back and enjoy the blood circulating through my system. I felt a renewed vigour start to build. There was nothing akin to human blood – Priest was right in that it told stories like no other. Animal blood merely gave me an incoherent fleeting flash here and there. The blood I had just ingested had many stories to tell. All manner of emotions flowed through my veins. An explosive high began to build and build until I felt something that could only be likened to the temporary ecstasy felt in the throes of passion – something I had only experienced through the blood of others.

Worried that Priest could detect my thoughts, I cleared my mind and focused my attention on my new companion. He was sitting patiently and watching my every move intently. I gazed upon him with fresh eyes, filmy layer gone and vision restored. He was handsome, seemingly in his late thirties, dark hair slicked back into a neat bun, and opalescent grey eyes. He reminded me of someone I once held dear and his familiarity gave me the courage I needed. I could not help but seek answers to questions I so desperately sought from my captive audience.

"You have questions. Please speak freely; you are safe here."

I started with the one thing I had struggled most with. "Tell me then, Priest, are we evil?"

Slightly taken aback, he responded, "What makes you ask such a question?"

"Well, what thing drinks blood as we do?"

"Why, there are many species of animal that drink the blood of humans. Is it so strange that it nourishes and sustains our life? We are hemovores – just another type of human. A mutation if you will. Doesn't human science speak of such things?" He spoke as if he knew all things, but his answer was not quite good enough.

"But I kill when I feed," I argued, incredulous.

"Many animals kill without remorse. One must survive. It is vital for a balanced life cycle, or the natural ebb and flow of life, if you will."

"They do not know it is wrong. I have no excuse as I have the mental capacity to understand that it is inherently wrong."

"Against what standards are you measuring this? Who is to say what is right and what is wrong? I exist, you exist, and we survive how we must."

"But you are a priest – do you not care?"

"I do. These are but questions I pose to you to gain a better understanding of your state of mind. You must do what pleases you."

"Then I must die."

He gently placed his hand on mine and took a deep breath. There was empathy in his eyes for me.

"You suffer needlessly. You must embrace your nature, but in a way that does not conflict with your beliefs. You may drink from a willing human, but that is difficult without revealing yourself; you may drink from animals if you consider their worth less than yours; you may take from a donor bank; you may drink little and often from humans, ensuring they do not die and that they do not exchange blood with you or another like us."

"I struggle to see why anyone would want to burden a human with this sickness. What would be the use of such an action?"

"There are many reasons, usually companionship. I am sure there were times when you wished for someone special. Perhaps that is why you were changed."

"Surely not. I am no use to anyone. I have nothing to offer."

"I assure you that you do," he whispered, almost as if he felt pain from the words that I uttered. I suddenly wanted to know more about this man. What suffering did he hide under his smooth exterior which had been shaken by a simple statement? For the first time since my dark awakening, my thirst for knowledge was stronger than my desire to feed.

I cleared my parched throat and asked, "Have you ever changed a human, Priest?"

"No, I have no desire to," he answered quickly. I sensed reluctance, but it had been years since I had shared words with someone and I had missed conversation.

"Have you ever exchanged blood after your transformation?"

"I have only received from Draconis himself, as he is the one who changed me. He also sacrifices his blood during ceremonies to grace his children with a drop of his strength."

"What was it like?"

"Well, remember I told you that blood tells a more powerful story than a religious text? Blood serves other purposes besides sustenance. We also use it as a form of communication. The stories his blood told were full of a rich, violent history. I feel honoured to have tasted his life."

Seeing my body droop and sag, he held another bag of blood out to me. "Here, you must drink. Your strength has faded greatly."

Realising that the wave of euphoria had faded as heroine fades from the human body, I eyed the second bag lustfully.

Forgetting myself, I took it and devoured the blood greedily. Priest sat and watched me closely, clearly curious and longing to ask questions of his own. He had been polite up until now, patiently answering the multitude of questions – some of them personal, despite my comments being laced with disdain and disbelief at first.

After I had drained every drop of blood, he asked, "May I ask you a question? Why have you neglected yourself?" He sat expectantly. It was his turn now.

Although I was tempted to tell him to leave me be, I had to return some of the courtesy he showed me. Taking a deep breath, I replied, "I destroyed those I professed to love."

He leaned in a little closer, close enough that I could clearly see his piercing silvery-grey eyes. "Why did you first run away from the family home?"

I felt panic rise as I vigorously shook my head. "It is a pain too great to speak of and I wish to speak of it no further."

He now placed both hands on mine. "I understand that it is difficult, but what you fail to accept is that you suffered at the hands of your parents. The bloodlust brings out the rage that we have suppressed. That is partly why you suffered as you have."

I was muted by his intuition, his wisdom, and the harsh truths he uttered. I grasped my head in vain, trying to let the fresh wave of anguish run its course. Memories of abuse that I had buried so deep started to emerge. I had always blamed myself for what had happened.

"I just wanted to be loved," I whispered.

"Perhaps that is why your maker chose you. Nightwalkers are attracted to pain. It makes the blood taste all the more intense and full-bodied."

Had I always been that transparent? Had I been walking around with my pain on display for the world to see? "I did not mean to kill them."

"They deserved a fate worse than death. You showed mercy by drinking them dry. You should have been loved by your maker, nurtured, and moulded in preparation for your new life. In your confusion, you sought out familiarity, and you were drawn to what you knew. You were drawn to suffering."

"Suffering? It was love I yearned for." A hot tear spilled down my check. "And what of my brother?" I asked.

"He may not understand, but you saved him."

Priest left me with my own tumultuous thoughts after informing me that a room had been prepared for me. I did not move from my spot until the breaking of dawn loomed ever closer. Finally, I made my way to the small room and saw that clean clothes and a towel had been left on the bed, and the window had been boarded up to combat the rays of impending doom.

Darkness was a welcome release as I slept.

JUDGEMENT

Entering the council chamber set my nerves on fire. It was time to get the answers that Priest did not know the answers to. I sat on a lone chair placed in the middle of a circle of chairs. One by one, the council members entered wearing black ceremonial robes. After resting and washing, I hoped my appearance was acceptable. As advised by Priest, I averted my vision downwards to appear respectful.

Arriving later than all the others was a figure clad in red. He appeared to be a man in his forties with a beautiful, silky mane of jet black hair and the darkest eyes I had ever seen. I would have once envied his hair, but my lack of self-care was evident. He almost seemed familiar, but I was sure I would have remembered this striking man, who I assumed was Draconis.

Once seated, the council proceeded to ask me a series of questions and they deliberated as if I were not there. All the while, Draconis did not utter one word. Priest stood off to the side awaiting their verdict. They wrote their votes down on paper and handed them to Draconis who read each one, tallying up the result. He looked up, making eye contact with me for the first time. His piercing gaze stabbed through me, sending a cold chill down my spine. Just for a moment, I sensed hesitation, but it quickly disappeared. He stood to deliver the verdict.

"Young one, how you have lived your life, broken and afraid. Now you have your wish. Now you can die. You will have peace."

"I don't want to die," I gasped, shocked by my own admission. For the first time in my undead life, I felt fear. Odd that now my fate lay in the hands of another, I felt the will to survive. I wanted to live. How ungrateful I had been. Every life is worth living. If I was not meant to be, then how come I exist?

"You are the illegitimate offspring of a law-breaking nightwalker. The law is clear on this matter," he coldly stated.

"But I was turned against my will through no fault of my own."

"Yet, what did you do with your gift? You begged for death and now your wish is granted. Isn't that a comfort to you? You no longer have that burden to bear. Your life will end and there will be no painful recovery from yet another failed suicide attempt."

I was about to respond again, but before I could, Draconis raised his hand authoritatively and said, "Enough. Priest, escort her to the prison chamber. This meeting is adjourned."

The cell door closing appeared to symbolise the end of my life.

"How could you stand by and do nothing? You did not tell me you were bringing me to my death."

"I had believed that they would see sense. Their judgement is no reflection of your character or the value of your worth." He took a deep breath as if battling his own feelings. "It is expected that I obey the wishes of the council."

"You helped restore my faith and for that, I will be ever grateful. I thought God had abandoned me, but perhaps Satan has a plan for me. And I haven't yet had a chance to realise my destiny. It can't end like this!"

"But what would you do differently, Aurora, tell me? You have done nothing but wallow in despair for sins that you did not commit." His scathing words cut me to the bone as I knew them to be true. I'd had a second chance and I had thrown it away.

"I would find a purpose as you did, Priest. I could atone for my sins. I would save those who suffered as I did – the homeless and unsheltered from the burden of human suffering and addiction. I will find a purpose, one way or another."

He shook his head in defeat. "Priest? How can you blindly follow this verdict? Surely you hold your own judgement? Who are they to tell you that your judgement is redundant?" I let my words sink in.

After a while, he raised his eyes and said, "You do not have to plead your case to me. Please forgive my remarks. I wanted to see if your intentions were pure. From the start, I could see that you had merely lost your way. You are indeed right – my feelings on the matter must determine my actions. You should not be punished for a crime that you did not commit. I will aid your escape. I will put your safety in the hands of my most trusted confidant, a human, who is most dear to me. A true man of the cloth. But you must promise me that you will not drink from him or reveal your dark gift. He will keep you safe and hidden. I will do all I can to prevent the council from pursuing you."

"Thank you, Priest. Your compassion knows no bounds."

"It is the least I can do for putting you in such a precarious position. Please forgive me for my lack of foresight." He opened the unlocked cell door and he stepped back, allowing me to walk through.

Impulsively, I pulled him into a tight embrace. I felt his heart beat powerfully against mine. The warmth of his body exuded safety and protectiveness. I wanted to hold on to this security for longer, but the moment came to a halt when he awkwardly cleared his throat and said, "We should hurry. Time is of the essence."

Taking my hand, he led me further into the cavernous dungeon that lay beneath the council chamber. How he found his way through the pitch-black tunnels, I had no idea, but I blindly followed along. I had no choice but to put my trust in this man – a man who I had grown fond of. We walked until we were faced with a crack in the wall, which could not quite block out the pale light of the moon peeking through.

Effortlessly, he removed the rock and led me down narrow steps. Seeing a boat docked ahead, I knew what he had in mind. It was a clever way to ensure that I could not be tracked. A man, who was similarly clad, was waiting for me in the boat.

"Bastian, this is Aurora. It is of utmost importance that you keep her safe as we discussed." So, Priest had not lacked foresight after all. Although he had genuinely hoped that the council would make a fair judgement, he had made alternative plans if the situation were to go awry.

"Father, what is this all about? Why the urgency? Should we approach the authorities for guidance?"

"I will explain all someday, my friend. Please trust me as you always have."

"Okay, Aurora. Please sit and be safe." He gave my hand one last squeeze, making me fear for his life. I hoped he had not put himself on the line. I had selfishly questioned his judgement without thinking of the possible ramifications. What would happen to him should the council find out that he aided and abetted my escape? I was dreadfully afraid for his safety. Fearing for the life of another was something I had not felt in a very long time. It awoke old feelings, long buried and forgotten from a past life.

"Please be careful," I pleaded.

"No, you be careful. Do not worry about me," he ordered, as he pushed the boat forward.

Bastian eyed me warily as he pushed and pulled the oars, his breathing becoming increasingly more laboured. I could feel the blood flowing in his veins, but I had to honour my promise to Priest. I would have to take whatever opportunity I could to find food, considering that I was still recovering from my self-neglect. Suspicion marred his features, as well as concern for Priest's welfare.

We eventually arrived at the jetty and Bastian hastily boarded with me in tow, whilst scanning our surroundings. The sun was set to rise shortly. I could see his dedication to Priest, carrying out his orders dutifully, despite the peculiar nature of the request. His dedication alone was enough to convince me that Priest was indeed a good man. I had never known one previously.

Once outside our cabins, he instructed me not to leave my room and explained that he would be next door if there was an emergency of any kind. He disappeared into his room and I knew that he expected me to do the same. Sitting on my bed, I thought about Priest and dearly hoped that he was okay, as the guilt grew in my gut.

Three days of hunger.

Three days of catching every rat I could find.

In my weakened state, I yearned for blood. Even when Bastian came to check on me, my eyes settled on his neck and my heart beat faster in anticipation of the taste. I reminded myself of my promise to Priest and told him to leave immediately. He left without question and I wondered if he knew my dark secret after all. Priest had put his faith in me and I had to prove that I was worth saving. Despite my erratic behaviour, Bastian proved to be a loyal companion, regularly monitoring me. Although I did not quite provide the information he probed for, he still kept his word and he carried out his task as well as he could.

AWAKENING

On the third night, we reached our destination. Priest was waiting for me at the dock and immediately, I was relieved. I felt my heart beat quicken when he smiled warmly at me, but that did not stop me from holding him in a fierce embrace. He held me tightly against his chest, equally relieved. My heart quickened and my gums throbbed due to a sudden and overwhelming urge to drink his blood, but not in the usual way. I assumed I was disorientated from the lack of food. Embarrassingly, when he kissed me lightly on the neck, I found that my fangs had extended in response. When we separated, his dilated eyes bored into mine and I felt that he could sense my desire.

"You are safe, Aurora," he whispered, whilst he stroked my cheek tenderly.

"Thank you for all of this and I am sorry for doing this to you; for ruining your life."

"And I would do it one hundred times over. There is something about you that I could not bear to see extinguished by a hasty judgement. I also feel that we have a lot more to share." I felt almost giddy with excitement, like a young child.

Realising that Bastian had watched the whole scene between us unfold, I broke the embrace, feeling self-conscious about my highly unusual display of affection. He looked on curiously.

"Bastian, I cannot thank you enough. I am forever in your debt."

"I don't understand what this is all about, Priest."

"In time, my friend, in time. Now go and continue your good work. Do not concern yourself with this matter any longer." And with that, he turned and left, fading away into the darkness.

"We must hurry before the sun rises," Priest warned, as we went to board yet another rowing boat.

He rowed in silence into nothingness and never-ending blackness. I watched as Priest rowed without tiring, determination set on his face. The full moon edged its way above the horizon, spreading its ghostly light upon the ripples in the water. The light reflected in Priest's eyes and I felt drawn to the intensity of his gaze as he made eye contact with me. How old his character seemed to be, yet how young his features appeared to be. I could detect a hidden intelligence in the bottomless depths of his black pupils. What kind of man had he been when human? He would have been an impressive specimen, even then.

Surprising myself with thoughts of love and wishes of affection, I looked down in shame. Guilt had taken root inside me like a venomous plant. I thought of all the people I had killed due to my inability to control my urges. Perhaps, I was a foul creature who deserved to live in the subterranean underbelly of the human world, hidden in shadow and in darkness.

I was pulled out of my miserable reverie when I detected land in the distance. I saw bats circling about, indicating a food source nearby. How fitting, I thought to myself, bemused by the irony. The closer we came, the more I could make out the terrain. It was an island with sand that appeared grey in the moonlight. I clumsily stumbled out, forgetting my weakened state, and I was steadied by strong hands. Bizarrely, I suddenly felt gaunt and unattractive. I had once been considered beautiful in my human days, but I wondered what Priest must think of me now.

"How will I feed here, Priest?" I was almost afraid to ask. I did not want to be even more of a burden to him with my selfish needs.

"You will feed from me for now. You are still too weak to hunt large game, so I will hunt and you will drink from me."

"But, it would weaken you, would it not?"

"No, I will use the blood of animals, be them large or small, to maintain my strength."

We stopped at what appeared to be a doorway at the side of a mountain, camouflaged by moss. Priest moved it aside and led me into a cramped tunnel that opened out to a small space. It was a room, set up much like a living space. It was simple and crude, but to me, it was luxury. He handed me the torch, while he set up a small, controlled fire in the centre of the room.

"The sun will rise shortly, Aurora, but you will be safe from the sun's rays here. I will sleep on the floor by the exit tunnel and you may use the bedded area in the far corner."

Using his bag as a pillow, he settled by the gaping hole. I, in turn, lay down on the makeshift mattress, which was padded with straw. It was heaven compared to the pile of rubble I had used as a resting place for many years.

When I awoke from my fitful sleep, full of nightmares and forgotten memories, it took me a moment to adjust to my new surroundings. All was quiet, apart from the soft, even sound of Priest's breathing. I stood by him, curiously watching his subconscious form. His hair had become loose and it splayed out, revealing a thin strand of silver, which I had not noticed before. He certainly was an impressive man.

I knelt down, lost in studying his fascinating features and admiring his muscular form. Unexpectedly, he opened his eyes, looking directly at me as if he had detected my presence all along.

"Good morning. I trust you slept well?" I reared back, startled.

"Sorry, I lost myself for a moment there."

Shifting to a sitting position, he said, "I can see that you are in desperate need of blood. It explains your confusion. Come, you must feed."

I tentatively sat down beside him and motioned for me to come closer.

"Do not be afraid. I will not harm you," he reassured. "Where do you desire to drink from?" he asked pointing to his neck and then his wrist. The vein in his neck throbbed and I saw nothing else.

A moment later, my teeth were piercing his flesh and liquid silk invaded my senses. He resisted my probing thoughts, but I persisted and pushed through the veil. I saw a woman's face, I felt her soft lips and I felt his love and desire for her. I saw the same woman in a coffin and he was crying. His maker found him on his knees, grief-stricken and on the edge of life in the cemetery. All hope lost, his pain was a beacon. He had suffered the same as I. The vision changed and I saw how he saw me – red hair, wild and fiery; green eyes, the colour of peridot, with flecks of emerald. I was beautiful in his eyes. He desired to free me of my pain. The vision faded.

"That is enough now, Aurora."

I opened my eyes to find that I held him in a lover's embrace astride his lap. "My saviour, you suffer too," I whispered huskily. I reached out to stroke his face and he closed his dilated eyes, inhaling my scent. I never knew how incredibly intimate it was to share blood with another nightwalker. I noticed his teeth extending as mine had the night before.

He took my hand in his, held it gently, and responded, "I did once, Aurora. I did not mean for you to see that, but I could not hide it from you."

Something that can only be described as a human emotion overcame me. I lifted his chin and kissed him tenderly on his warm lips. To my surprise, he did not recoil and returned my gesture. Stunned with the realisation of what a privilege that had been, I detached myself from him, hand on my pounding heart.

I could not deny that I felt love for him. I longed for love's warm embrace, but was it possible for a creature such as me? How could he love me?

I once believed that I was spawn born from the seed of hell itself, and I had chosen to unleash my dark and deadly power. How could I atone for that? I wanted to rip out my heart so I no longer felt this. I wanted to be rid of guilt's toxic grasp.

A sob escaped me before I could suppress it. I doubled over, trying to breathe through my regret. In an instant, Priest was there, holding me. We dropped to our knees, falling beside one another.

"I do not deserve to be loved or saved. Every person I drained from, I felt nothing for. I should be cursed with this retched life for all eternity."

Grabbing hold of my shoulders, Priest shook me vigorously. "Look at me! You did not choose this life and your master did not teach you. Think about the people you say you murdered. You chose them for a reason."

I felt the vehemence of his conviction, but it did little to comfort me. "Even if they were consumed with ill intent, what right did I have to decide their fate? Who am I to judge who may live or die?"

"The human world would never have dealt the appropriate punishment for these creatures. You did humanity a great service by ridding the world of such scum. You did not choose blindly like an animal," he insisted.

Rendered speechless by the severity of his words and the extent to which he defended me, I did not respond immediately. I wanted to believe his words, but I could not. I shook my head doubtfully.

Finally, I said, "I am scum also. I am as worthless as they."

"No, Aurora. Not to me. You have filled a hollowness that took root in my core ever since the day my beloved, Anne, died."

He guided my face upwards so that I faced him. He leaned his forehead against mine and we listened to one another breathe. After some time, we breathed in rhyme.

We were one.

***

The moon and stars shone brightly in the inky sky above, illuminating the land, and shimmering on the sea while Priest went to feed. I needed to cleanse myself of impurities and the sea awaited. Time slipped away as my body, now warm with Priest's blood, adjusted to the cold water. Soon, it felt soothing against my bare skin as I moved further in. Sliding the soap over my skin, I thought of Priest, my saviour and my protector. Without him, I would have nothing. I was afraid to lose him. I knew that I wanted to live if only to be near him. I wanted him more than any drug, more than blood itself.

I wanted to give him the only gift that I could.

Gathering my courage, I called out to him when he returned from hunting. He came running, afraid for my safety, perhaps thinking that we had been found. "Do not worry. I only want you to join me."

He shook his head, unsure of how to respond. "I cannot..."

"I am afraid too, but I do not know how long I shall live and I want to share with you what I can as a gesture of gratitude. I wish to offer my blood to you, so that you may know me too."

"But you are weakened still."

"I am fine. My strength is returning. Will you do me the honour?"

"You offer it freely?" he asked in disbelief.

"Of course. As you offered yours. I do not wish to waste what is left of my life. One day they will find us, be it tomorrow or years to come, so why not experience this before it is too late." Seeing that he made no move, I continued, "Your powerful aura surrounds me. I feel your pain and suffering. I am drawn to your darkness and I crave it. Now come with me. Know me before I die."

"I am afraid."

"It is I who is more afraid." I turned my body, my back facing him, beckoning him no further to leave the decision entirely in his hands.

A moment later, I heard him remove his clothing and enter the water. My heart fluttered as I felt his hand upon my shoulder and his hot breath against my damp neck. I felt one hand glide across my waist and the other swept my hair to one side. I closed my eyes in anticipation, awaiting his bite. He pulled me close against his naked form and sunk his fangs deep into the cradle of my neck. I felt a pleasurable pain as they pierced my skin. I entered a trance-like state and swooned as if I were drunk.

I lost all awareness of space and time while he explored me, but it was abruptly cut short when he released me and I awakened in his arms.

Breathing deeply, he gasped, "You have dragon's blood." Those were the last words I had expected to hear and it took me more than a moment to comprehend the enormity of his discovery.

"What? How can this be?"

"This scandal, this treachery originates in the heart of the council itself. Don't you see? Only council members have dragon's blood – a gift from the dark lord himself. It flows through them only. We must return to London and face them. We must plead our case and expose the culprit. A pardon must be given to us. You are right – we cannot run forever."

CONFESSION

They tracked us down as we neared the dock. Rain pelted down, but through the droplets, I saw them. Hooded figures, standing in unison, awaited our departure. Blood-thirsty, reflective eyes revealed their true intentions. Hunger and desire emanated strongly from them.

"I see that you have come to surrender, friend," one said to Priest.

"I am glad that you saw sense and now seek our wise counsel," a second added.

"Perhaps he will forgive you," another sniggered.

Barely veiled menace surrounded us as we were led to the council chambers. Priest took my hand in a sign of unity, which they sneered on. Such displays of affection were most likely frowned upon as they signified weakness. We entered the building and walked towards our doomed fate. Stepping through the arched doorway, we knew that there would be no escape. This time, we both stood in the centre to await the arrival of the all mighty, Draconis.

"We are gathered here, my most trusted companions, to deliver our verdict and carry out the most severe of punishments. It brings me no pleasure to sentence my child, a once valued member of the council, but he has strayed from us. The lure of human nature was all too enticing."

"Draconis, we are innocent. Hear us. She has dragon's blood," Priest pleaded.

"If this is the case, then Draconis will decide her fate," the tall, dark-skinned council member said, reminding us of our place.

Daring to be bold, I said, "Draconis, I offer you my blood." A flicker of uncertainty, which was almost imperceptible, flashed in his eyes. "Surely, you are not afraid to drink?"

He quickly recovered. "You do not need to offer it, my child, as I will take it if I deem necessary. I do not require permission from you. I have no hesitance, so I do not understand what fear you speak of."

"If there is a traitor among us who does not respect our law, we must weed him out!" the pale one shouted.

Taking a step forward, I moved my hair aside and offered him my neck. His eyebrows rose. "So brazen, my child. I see that Priest has not schooled you in our ways." He took my hand, turned it around, and bit into my wrist, choosing not to drink from my neck. At first, he wrinkled his nose as if some foul taste displeased him. Withdrawing his fangs after barely tasting a drop, he turned to face the council. "Preposterous. No such thing. It is untrue," he declared.

I looked at the elders' faces in disbelief. Surely, Priest had not been mistaken?

"Priest?" I said helplessly, looking up at him for an answer I did not have. He looked down, equally perplexed. Suddenly, the silence was broken as he gasped in realisation.

"The only reason you lie, oh great leader, is because your own blood flows through her veins. *You* are her maker!" Priest accused. He turned to face the council. "I call for a vote of no confidence!"

It was at this moment, that the fragility of the council was made clear. Their distrust of one another was plain to see, as well as their desire for power. Draconis was not as admired as he thought himself to be. He had enemies among his own beloved, handpicked brood. It was fear that had made them obey so willingly.

"Is there any weight to this accusation?" the small dark-haired one asked.

"There is only one way to find out. We all must taste her blood given the gravity of this situation."

Every one of them inched closer and closer, like vultures drawn to a carcass. No matter what front or air they tried to convey, they were nothing but blood-thirsty creatures, and as common as any cretin roaming an alleyway. The only difference was that these individuals hid behind their neatly pressed robes. They converged on me until all I could see was blackness and all I could feel were a dozen sharp sets of teeth devouring me. My blood burned as it was taken from me against my will. The pain was excruciating, yet I did not protest.

Once they had their way with me, I lay in a heap, weakened by all the blood loss. Priest broke through the congregation and fell by my side, weeping.

As I lay broken, hovering on the edge of life, I willed Priest to abandon me.

"Here, drink from me," Priest choked.

"No, let the council do with me as they will. Let them destroy me. You must survive and thrive without me. You are a good man and you do not deserve this."

"But I was not always good. I once stood on the council and passed severe sentences upon poor innocents. Not once did I try to stop it and the guilt that festers is unbearable." Even in my weakened state I was surprised by his admission, as I had not seen this during our blood share. Now I understood why we had been drawn to one another. "That is why I left the council to carry out good deeds. We can both atone for our sins now."

My condition did not stop the meeting from proceeding. "So, it is true," a female voice spat. "You are a blood-addicted fiend, no better than sewer scum. The rumours are true. It was you who went on adulterous feeding frenzies to satiate your voracious appetite."

"How dare you speak to me with such contempt! I am Draconis. I am your leader and I will decide my fate. I made you and I gave you the honour of serving me."

"Contempt? You do not even deny the accusation. I was right to suspect you. How dare you make a mockery of our code, a code that was designed to protect us. You put us all in danger, frivolously flirting with danger. Consider how many countless and nameless nightwalkers you sentenced to death. All so you could have a taste to gratify your desire. Exchanging of blood is reserved for the most sacred of rituals."

"Are we not all guilty of this crime? Even our virtuous Priest admitted to blood exchange with a rogue, who could have revealed all to the humans."

"No, this is not so. I plan to name her my life partner." Priest declared through his weeping. Upon hearing his words, I wept also. My only love had been blood and blood alone, but Priest awoke a part of me that I had long forgotten. He had saved me from myself. No matter what happened, his love would sustain me until the end of time, into eternity, and beyond.

Gaining confidence, the blond-haired male advanced on Draconis. "It was the thrill of blood exchange that spurred you. What of the bond you shared with your victims who perished at the hands of us. The illegitimate offspring of your unbridled bloodlust; the fruit of your drunken binge are lost and wander aimlessly in the night. We were blindly led astray and deceived by our illustrious leader. Perhaps now it is time for a new leader."

"Earth offers a generous bounty lush with human blood to feast on. Why shouldn't we reap such rewards?" Draconis argued, becoming increasingly desperate.

The dark-skinned one snorted scornfully. "If vampires were to rule, who would be left to feed on? Us? It would be a carnage too dreadful to comprehend. We would die in the barren wasteland that we created."

"I will change the law. Permission will no longer be needed to change others, so that you all may share this bounty. I was wrong to have only thought of myself." He was clutching at straws, it seemed.

"And the result? An army of undead, rampant and uninhibited. We are not savages! Changing the law just to make right your actions? You will not pull the wool over our eyes again. How will we ever trust you? How many times have you succumbed to this bloodlust? Most of us can control it but you, my *father*, cannot. Only a few are afflicted with such an addiction and I need not remind you that there is no cure," the one with long silver hair said, obviously enjoying the opportunity to humiliate his leader.

The tall dark one spoke. "We look to you for leadership but you disgrace us. I vote for a new leader. Those who agree, raise your hand."

Even through my blurred vision, I could make out the hands of each and every member. Never had I seen a group so keen to rid themselves of their leader.

Despite this blatant display of mutiny, Draconis still continued to plead, "But that is not possible, I am the first."

"The first must put the needs of the many before their own."

Draconis fell to the ground in defeat. There was no way that he could overcome this great a number. "But I cannot die."

They encircled his cowering form, blocking any means of escape. As if Draconis were not present, they deliberated, eager to be rid of him. My vision faded further and the voices in the room became muffled and disjointed.

"Aurora! You must drink!" Priest cried out, voice full of anguish.

"No, let me die. I cannot atone for my sins because I cannot forgive myself." The truth was that a part of me had enjoyed it all. I was a monster.

"I will not stand by and accept that! If you die, then I will ask the council to kill me also." I heard a tearing sound as if flesh had been ripped apart. Warm blood dripped onto my parched lips. Priest held his wrist closer so that I would choke on it if I did not swallow. I did not have the strength to resist. I gave in to his request and drank.

Clouded visions of Priest as a young man consumed me, and once again, I yearned to experience his sadness, his joy, and his pain. I wished to re-live each memory with him, and I was ready to share the past that I had avoided for so long. After some time, my hearing had returned somewhat, and I willed myself to stop drinking, despite the temptation to continue exploring. When I opened my eyes, Priest's face, full of love and concern, looked upon me. His features had become gaunt from blood loss, yet he was beautiful still.

"I am so sorry, I took too much blood. You need to feed."

"We both need to feed, my love, but for now, we have enough and we have each other," he said, just before placing a tender kiss on my blood-stained lips. He collapsed beside me.

The council's viperous words were spat upon Draconis as they decided his fate. Why had he created the law, only to disregard it entirely? Why had he created me, a bastard child, only to discard me? He had betrayed me and others like me. I thought of those that I had mercilessly killed. I may not have committed those heinous acts if I had been nurtured during my vampire infancy. He was but a poor imitation of what a leader, or a father, was meant to be.

"Draconis, we have come to a decision. We will drink your life essence and share this power. We will be the new elder," the small one declared theatrically, although Draconis had clearly heard every word of their deliberation.

"That will not stop me. I will hunt you down. I will destroy all of you. You! Traitorous seed of my blood!"

The pale one stepped forward with a sneer. "When we have finished feasting on your flesh, we will dissect you into twelve pieces and each piece is to be placed in the highest of mountains, the deepest of seas, and the darkest of canyons by each of us. If you survive, you will exist in limbo until we see fit to release you. You will lie dormant until you are awoken from your displaced slumber."

"You underhanded, disloyal, and spineless spawn of my own flesh! You always sought to destroy me so that you could lead, but I warn you, you will fail. Without my wisdom, you will expire, not by the hands of the humans, but by your brothers and sisters. You are doomed to fail. After you have all but perished, I will remain until the end of time," Draconis warned ominously.

"So be it, Father."

The council stalked him as they would their prey, something feral and primal taking over. It seemed as if they had patiently bided their time over the millennia until an opportune moment presented itself. He had given his children a taste of his blood and now they wanted for more – more than he was willing to give. He struggled, but there were too many to fight, despite his power.

Whilst they dealt their deadly punishment, we slunk away quietly into the shadows. As we neared the exit, to our freedom, screams of agony echoed down the long dark tunnels. They became less and less frequent and faded into nothingness. No one hunted us for now. The council would be consumed with their newfound power for quite some time.

"Priest? What if we cannot purify ourselves from the sins that we have committed?"

"Then we will face eternal damnation and the burning fires of hell together," he whispered resolutely. Oddly, that gave me great comfort.

The cold, unforgiving night air signified our freedom, albeit temporarily, as I suspected that we had made enemies. Draconian sympathisers may very well crawl out of the woodwork, intent on unleashing their judgement and wreaking their revenge. We did not know what challenges the future would bring; though, one thing was certain in this life: immortality comes at a price.

Do not wish for it.

ABOUT THE AUTHOR

From a young age, L. F. Gobin discovered a creative flair, which manifested itself primarily through art. Over the years, her creative thirst then branched out into poetry with a somewhat dark theme. Later on in life, L. F. Gobin developed a passion for photography and jewellery making.

Now, she is writing fiction for adults and children. Her novellas, Rogue (supernatural horror), and Missing (fantasy), are now available to read.

Find out more about L. F. Gobin here:
https://lfgobin.wixsite.com/obsidianplanet